THE POSTMAN'S DOG

story by
LISA SHANAHAN

pictures & design by
WAYNE HARRIS

ALLEN&UNWIN

For Scott and Simone,
with love and thanks for the journey.
And for Emily, and her journey just begun — L.S.

For Pete — W.H.

First published in 2005

Allen & Unwin, 83 Alexander St, Crows Nest NSW 2065, Australia
Phone: (61 2) 8425 0100   Fax: (61 2) 9906 2218
Email: info@allenandunwin.com   Web: www.allenandunwin.com

National Library of Australia
Cataloguing-in-Publication entry:

Shanahan, Lisa.
The postman's dog.

For children.
ISBN 1 74114 252 0.

1. Letter carriers - Juvenile fiction. 2. Dogs - Juvenile fiction.
I. Harris, Wayne. II. Title

A823.3

Cover and text design by Wayne Harris
Set in Fritz
Printed in China by Everbest Printing Co

10 9 8 7 6 5 4 3 2 1

The illustrations for this book were created digitally.

Charlie was a very good postman.
Every morning he got up
before the sun and began his run.

He loved the crinkle of cellophane and
the feathery lightness of overseas mail.

But most of all he loved people.

He always had time
to have a crumpet
with Mr Kumaradeva
and his afghan Holly.

He liked to hang out
a load of sheets
for Miss Zielinski
and Quincy,
her labradoodle.

He couldn't help
plucking weeds
with Mr Tran and
his silky terrier Dragon.

And his day wasn't done
until he had shared a joke
with Francesca and
Don the dalmatian.

Charlie was the most
well loved and well licked
postman in town.

Every afternoon,
Charlie sat on the
front porch with his wife
and told her stories
about his day.

He told her about
Mr Kumaradeva
with all of his family
in India.

He told her about
Miss Zielinski
singing opera in front
of the Queen.

He told her about
Mr Tran
and his journey
in a leaky boat.

He told her about
Francesca
starting ballet and
her new baby
brother Ryan.

And every night
he said,
"I've got the best job
in the world!"

But one day Charlie's wife died.

Charlie stopped
getting up
before the sun.

He stopped
chatting as he
delivered the mail.

And everywhere
he went mail got
mixed up and lost.

"He needs an afghan,"
said Mr Kumaradeva
to Miss Zielinski.

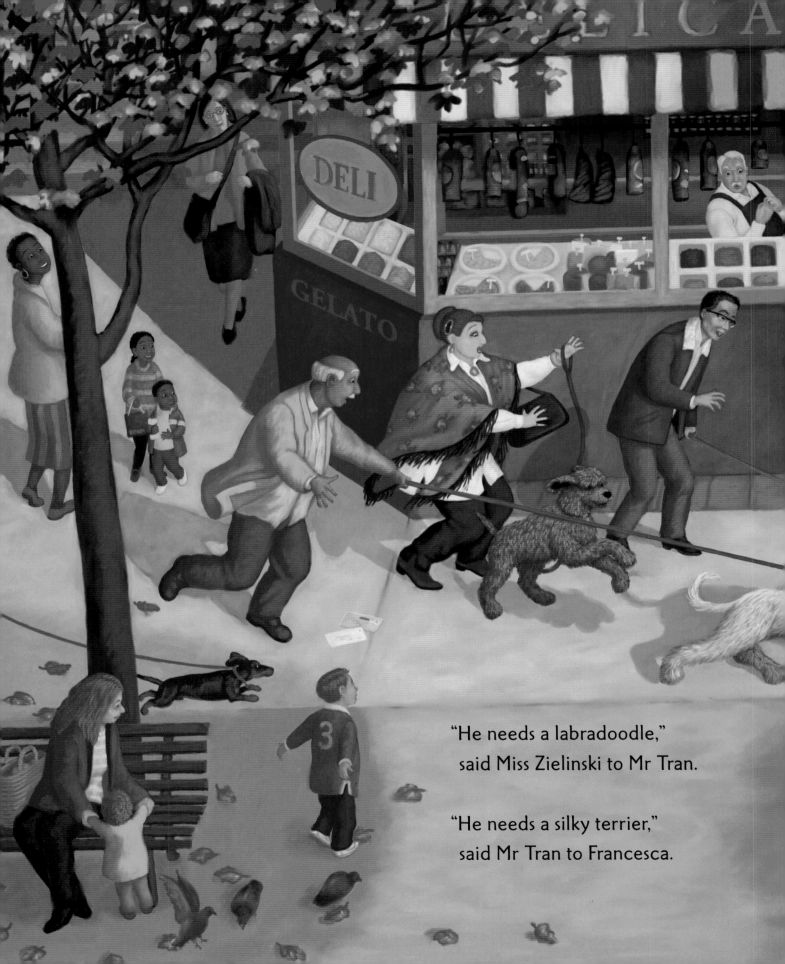

"He needs a labradoodle,"
said Miss Zielinski to Mr Tran.

"He needs a silky terrier,"
said Mr Tran to Francesca.

"You need a doggie with spots,"
shouted Francesca to Charlie
as he rode past,
"to give you licks and hugs."

So one morning Charlie
went to the dog pound.

He looked at dogs
with fat tails,
long, licky tongues,
tubby bottoms and
mournful, droopy jowls.

He saw snappy dogs
and happy dogs.
He patted tall dogs
and small dogs.

And just when he was
about to give up, he saw Lucy.

"What's she like?"
he nodded.

"She's a bitsa,"
said Violet, the vet.
"And her tail is bent.
But she's very calm.
The quietest dog
we've ever had."

"I'll take her,"
Charlie said.

That night Charlie
took Lucy for
a promenade in the park.

"She's so gentle,"
said Mr Kumaredeva.

"So peaceful!"
said Miss Zielinski.

"She's as tranquil as a paddy straw mushroom," said Mr Tran.

"She has the loveliest eyes," said Francesca.

Charlie took a long holiday.
Every morning he and Lucy
went for a walk.

Each day he washed
and combed
the burrs from her coat.

And every night
he sat on the porch and
told her his stories.

And before long,
Charlie felt hope tingle
across his skin
like soft, summer rain.

On his first day
back at work,
Charlie woke up
before the sun.

He took Lucy
for a walk,
ate his breakfast,
hummed in the shower
and hopped into his
postman's uniform.

But the moment
Lucy saw him,
her ears flicked up
and her fur bristled.

"RUFF! RUFF! RUFF!"
she barked.
"RUFF! RUFF! RUFF!"

"Shhhhhh,"
whispered Charlie.
"You'll wake up
Mrs Montague
next door."

But when Charlie
put on his helmet,
Lucy barked even louder.
"RUFF! RUFF! RUFF!"

And as he pedalled
up the street,
he could still
hear her barking.

When Charlie came
home that afternoon,
Lucy started up again.

"RUFF! RUFF! RUFF!"

And she didn't stop until
he took his uniform off.
Then she gave him a lick,
curled up in her basket
and wagged her tail.

"That dog of yours has got
a mighty loud bark,"
said Mrs Montague,
as Charlie took Lucy for
an evening walk.

"I know," said Charlie.

The next morning,
as soon as Charlie
put on his uniform,
Lucy barked.
"RUFF! RUFF! RUFF!"

Charlie took his
uniform off.

WAG! WAG! WAG!

He put it on.

"RUFF! RUFF! RUFF!"

He took it off.

WAG! WAG! WAG!

He put it on.

"RUFF! RUFF! RUFF!"

And the lights
switched on
in all the houses
up and down
the street.

That day the
mail was late.

"Where is your smile,
my friend?"
asked Mr Kumaradeva.

"Your eyes are sad,"
said Miss Zielinski.

"Maa-aate!"
said Mr Tran.

"What's wrong?"
asked Francesca.

"It's Lucy,"
whispered Charlie.
"She *hates* postmen."

That evening,
Mrs Montague
button-holed Charlie
on his evening walk.

"That dog," she said,
"is driving us MAD!"

"I'm sorry," said Charlie.

"You'll have to
do something,"
said Mrs Montague,
"before *someone*
calls the police."

The next morning
Charlie got dressed
on the front porch.

"Aaaaaaaaaaaaaaaah!"
screamed Mrs Montague.

Charlie bolted inside.
"RUFF! RUFF! RUFF!"

He bundled Lucy onto
the front of his bike.

"RUFF! RUFF! RUFF!"
she barked, as they
whipped up the drive.

"RUFF! RUFF! RUFF!"
she woofed, as he
picked up the mail.

"RUFF! RUFF! RUFF!"
she yapped, as he
delivered the post.

But when Charlie paused
to have a crumpet
with Mr Kumaradeva,
Lucy stopped barking.

And when Charlie
hung out the sheets
for Miss Zielinski,
Lucy's ears flicked down.

And while Charlie
plucked weeds
with Mr Tran,
Lucy's fur stopped bristling.

By the time Charlie
shared a joke
with Francesca,
Lucy's tail was swishing
and whishing.

The next morning,
Lucy woke up
before the sun.
She wagged her tail.

"RUFF! RUFF! RUFF!"
she barked.
And she didn't stop
until Charlie got up
and put on his uniform.

"Oh, Lucy," said Charlie
as they went whizzing
into the dawn,
"This is the best job
in the world."